We Bury the Landscape

An Exhibition-Collection

Kristine Ong Muslim

We Bury the Landscape

An Exhibition-Collection

Kristine Ong Muslim

Queen's Ferry Press

Queen's Ferry Press
8240 Preston Road
Suite 125-151
Plano, TX 75024
www.queensferrypress.com

The characters and events in this book are fictitious.
Any similarity to real persons, living or dead, is entirely
coincidental and not intended by the author.

Copyright © 2012 by Kristine Ong Muslim

All rights reserved, except for brief quotations in
critical articles or reviews. No part of this book may be
reproduced in any manner without prior permission from
the publisher: Queen's Ferry Press – 8240 Preston Road,
Suite 125-151, Plano, TX 75024

Published 2012 by Queen's Ferry Press

Cover art by Siobhan McCusker

First edition April 2012

ISBN 978-0-9839071-4-5

Printed in the United States of America

•Also by Kristine Ong Muslim•

Grim Series

Insomnia

Night Fish

Smaller Than Most

Graphic

A Roomful of Machines

Our Mr. Flip

·Advance Praise for *We Bury the Landscape*·

"Kristine Ong Muslim cultivates brilliance in her microfiction collection, *We Bury the Landscape*. Each of these mystical stories, inspired by a specific painting, have transformed into mesmerizing paintings themselves. Muslim delivers us into her own breathtaking museum with the extraordinary shifting shadows and light of dawn or dusk filtering into every piece—layer upon layer of thickly sculpted colors in language."

—Meg Tuite, author of *Domestic Apparition*

"Kristine Ong Muslim is that rare combination of playful imagination and gift for language. The depth of these gems, short as most are, astounds the reader. Yet there is also much humor, often in the face of despair. *We Bury the Landscape* is a book that you'll want to read again and again. Muslim is a writer you'll never forget."

—James Valvis, author of *How to Say Goodbye*

"*We Bury the Landscape* is a dynamic compilation of snapshot tales, each of which encompasses its own sensory-rich world and can be read in a few minutes or pondered for days. What's beautiful about the presentation here is that the collection is wholly nourishing and consumable in small, intense bites that intermingle on the palate and work together to fill the most intense literary craving."

—Jen Knox, author of *Musical Chairs* and *To Begin Again*

"*We Bury the Landscape* is an appropriate title for Kristine Ong Muslim's collection—the prose poems feel revealed. She has carefully hidden each poem for the reader to unearth: a treasure, startling and gorgeous."

—Valerie Loveland, author of *Reanimated, Somehow*

"Kristine Ong Muslim, with her collection of short-short stories and prose poems, comes to the table with something wholly new and fascinating. When reading each of the individual pieces, a whole begins to emerge, a complete tapestry of haunting, surrealist imagery, which is much larger than one initially suspects. One moment you are reading about a woman trying to create a visual landscape of her own, strange creatures, or the man who sleeps with his eyes open, and the next, almost before you realize it, you are side by side with the man inside what I can only hope is a perpetual dream. And all of this makes sense because you have already been drawn into the universe where both the literal and surreal have equal sway with the governing laws of existence. Muslim is able to produce an entire world in these stories/poems and here, as it has been my experience with Muslim's work in the past, her language is precise. Further, her use of imagery is marvelous in the best sense of the word and never is something expected or worn. Each story and poem is ekphrastic, based upon a painting, successfully pushing each written work to literally bridge the gap between the world and the visual landscape the narrator is trying to create."

—Justin Evans, author of *Town for the Trees* and editor of *Hobble Creek Review*

"After reading *We Bury the Landscape*, an ekphrastic flash fiction/prose poem collection by Kristine Ong Muslim, I'm convinced that voice is everything, and the voice in this book is both compelling and strong, unifying all the disparate, wonderful scenes. The writing is sure, a surrealist manifesto. Instead of simply reflecting the art, Muslim's pen leads the reader through extraordinary worlds, created by such singular artists as Joan Miró, Julie Heffernan, Peter Marcek, René Magritte, Jean-Marie Poumeyrol, among so many. In "House and Men," a work after *Wind* by Vladimir Kush, the Russian painter, Muslim writes, 'we are all versions of staircases at various angles,' a passage that gets at the brain of this stunning collection—giving life and breath to image. And she does that page after page."

—Sam Rasnake, author of *Inside a Broken Clock* and editor of *Blue Fifth Review*

"Reading *We Bury the Landscape* by the intimidatingly prolific Kristine Ong Muslim is like ingesting some bioluminescent lozenge & descending a lopsided staircase that shifts & breathes increasingly with each step. It's a precarious, hypnotic dance into the subliminal. Metamorphosis without metaphor. These ekphrastic prose poems are inhabited by a fairytale cast of elegantly macabre creatures: giant worms, plastic rabbits, murderous gryphons, carnivorous sunflowers, rubber Rapunzels, jars of aborted children, currency stashed in punctured skulls, honey seeping from severed wrists. There's an almost casual acceptance of the onion-like levels of inhabiting that we become witness to: dreams trapped within minds, minds within decaying bodies, bodies within crumbling dreamscapes. At heart, these are off-kilter snapshots of impermanence & the private godless apocalypse that's certain for us all. As we begin our descent, please keep your arms & legs inside the ride at all times."

—Scott Alexander Jones, author of *One Day There Will Be Nothing to Show That We Were Ever Here*

"*We Bury the Landscape* is a collection of ekphrastic vignettes set against surreal backdrops fraught with eerie characters faking normalcy. Kristine Ong Muslim's visceral prose poems slash the air with 'the precision of a matador's sword striking bone'—no reader can plunge into her multiverse without kissing their comfort zone goodbye."

—Arlene Ang, author of *Seeing Birds in Church is a Kind of Adieu*

"Like some of the artists whose work inspired this collection, Kristine Ong Muslim is herself a masterful creator not only of landscapes or portraits, but of parallel worlds complete with a surrealist, yet also strangely tangible, cast. The author expertly moves between reality and could-have-beens, nightmares and dreams. She slips inside the painter's skin, then confidently sheds it in possession of an entirely different truth. *We Bury the Landscape* is 'a barrelful of jack-in-the-box surprises,' sketches aimed at head, heart, and gut."

—Michaela A. Gabriel, author of *the secret meanings of greek letters*

"Reading Kristine Ong Muslim's work is like participating in an archeological dig. It is the landscape that draws us first, an unusual depression, that strange swirl of vegetation, a sudden, loamy softness in rocky terrain. And so we dig, trowel by trowel, micro-story by micro-story. We lose ourselves in the task of un-burying a bone fragment here, an artifact there. Posthumanism gives way to re-humanism. The inanimate breathes deep. Only when we have finished do we fully realize the skeleton we have unearthed is our own, reaching from the grave to touch our flesh, to feel the warmth we cast off so casually in our everyday lives. As entertaining as it is deep, *We Bury the Landscape* shines as an example of the flexible power of the micro-fiction form."

—Stephen V. Ramey, editor of the *Triangulation* anthologies

·Contents·

- 18· Landscape with Grenade
- 19· The Tilled Field
- 21· The People of the Farm
- 23· Bogomil's Landing
- 24· Bogomil's Ceremonial Stage: Caspar and His Props
- 26· Everything That Rises
- 28· Self-Portrait as Broken Home
- 29· Self-Portrait as World
- 30· Self-Portrait as Sky Scraper
- 32· Self-Portrait as Big House
- 33· Abandoned Dwellings
- 34· House and Men
- 35· Hope
- 36· For the One Who Got Away
- 37· Bad Egg
- 39· Cactus Man
- 40· The Spider
- 42· Nowhere Room
- 44· Gregor Samsa Plays the Flute

45•	The Misunderstood
47•	The Seashell
48•	The Adulterer
49•	Man in a Black Suit
51•	Moon Sonata
52•	Dryland
54•	The Collage Artist
56•	Birth of the Dream Monster
57•	Cow No. 7
58•	Revenge of the Goldfish
59•	The Ugly
60•	Birthday
62•	Evening Ceremonies
63•	What Better Lure
64•	Insomnias
65•	Damocles
66•	The Great Architect
67•	Giorgio at the Piazza
69•	This is a Headshot
70•	Colored Pencils
71•	The Red Orchestra
72•	Sphinx Embedded in the Sand
73•	Startled Emu

74·	The Dour Elephant-Kettle
75·	The Storyteller
76·	How the Invisible Man Gives Himself Away
77·	Obliterating the Outcast
78·	Milk Maiden
79·	A Much Younger Wife
80·	The Perilous Compassion of the Honey Queen
81·	Dangerous Liaisons
82·	The Couple in Lace
83·	René Magritte, the White Cloth, and the Lovers
85·	Birdcage
86·	Bad Love and Carnage
88·	The Village of the Mermaids
90·	Self-Portrait as Netherworld
92·	Self-Portrait as Roots
93·	Self-Portrait as Fiery Skirt
94·	Sketch for a Dirty Princess
97·	The First Days of Spring
98·	Bug Chairs
99·	One Story About Flight
100·	Rivalerne and Shelving
101·	Surgical Addiction
103·	A True Story

105•	Nobody's Beast
108•	The Taxidermist and the Girls Made of Dead Things
110•	Industrial Farm Family
112•	The Half-Mermaid
113•	Flowers, Secrets
116•	Rain of Men
117•	The Ladders
118•	Some Roses and Their Phantoms
119•	People from the Drop of Water
120•	Time Transfixed
121•	The Walking Lesson
122•	Bathyscaphe
123•	Underneath
124•	The City is Landing
126•	Attack at Dawn
127•	Prefab
128•	City of the Dead
130•	Inside the Calorimeter Cup
132•	As Long As You Burn
134•	Boy with a Propeller Head
136•	Tin Man Gets His Heart
137•	Requiem for Industry

139·	Shadow of a Boy
142·	The Apartment Building Before It Was Torn Down
144·	The First Horse Known to Men
146·	Landlocked
148·	Year of the Carnivores
150·	Strange City
151·	The car…
152·	The Gathering
153·	What the Boatman Sees
154·	Townscape
156·	Mirage
157·	We Figure the Leaves
160·	End of the World

Landscape with Grenade

after Cliff McReynolds' *Landscape with Grenade*

(1974)

oil on panel

When the little people discovered the grenade on their valley, they did not know what it was so they prayed to it, tilled the land and planted their tiny sacred crops around it as if it were some sort of shrine. Something so big and black with a curious contraption on one end had to beget miracles. So for months and months, they sang to it, asking for whatever it was little people desired in their little hearts. When nothing happened, they slit the throats of their little animals in sacrifice. And when nothing happened still, they pelted the grenade with small stones. The grenade-god, of course, would not budge.

The Tilled Field

after Joan Miró's *The Tilled Field* or *La terre labourée*

(1923 - 1924)

oil on canvas

66 × 92.7 cm

It took me two years to paint a view of my family's farm in Catalonia. It was difficult to select the right colors for a summer that never happened. I flattened the diorama; perspective would have given me away. Art historians might realize that I simply made everything up, and then I'd be back to square one—scamming tourists with "magic" jelly beans on the back roads of Montroig. You see the giant ear on the tree trunk? Some people concluded it had to do with my belief that objects have living souls. It was supposed to have been a leaf. And that eye on the tree? A fruit. This kind of mysticism brought out the paparazzi, the artsy crowd, the glut of gallery offerings I needed to make a living. And all those stylized creatures, like the burning horse, the entrapped squirrel, the hairless rooster, the elongated bull, etc., which were thought to have been inspired by medieval Spanish tapestries and

Catalan ceramics? Well, I admit to stenciling them right onto the canvas. The yellow was sunlight, representing hope. Truth is, I just ran out of green.

The People of the Farm

after Joan Miró's *The Farm*

(1921 - 1922)

oil on canvas

123.8 × 141.3 cm

There was a time when we could see through houses at will. We finally noticed amid the clutter whatever was broken and how it was impossible to fix.

There was a wheeled buggy that was always filled with corn for Elena to dehusk. In our time, it was always dawn, and she tried to delay completing her only chore by washing her hands in the communal pool. She dipped them in and out of the water as if drought was something that could not happen to people like us.

My village was mired in domesticity. We all took turns watering the sacred nettle in the middle of the town square. Suarez was the first of the farmhands to complain. I never heard from him again. Two days later, the compost pit intended for onions and tomatoes smelled so strongly that my father had to douse it with lime. He did not say a word. I did not have the stomach to ask.

We lived simple lives back then. What we pilfered, we returned in some other form. What seed pits we spat out, we buried in the ground so that they would grow into berries.

When I turned nineteen, I let everybody know that the chapel walls were beginning to show their age. God was not supposed to grow old. God was not supposed to get dirty like the rest of us. So we smeared ground eggshells mixed with paste on the cracks.

Every time it rained, we had to do it all over again.

Bogomil's Landing

after Otto Rapp's *Bogomil's Landing*

(1976 - 1992)

acrylic on canvas

23 3/4 × 32 in.

When Bogomil arrived on this planet, we gladly mistook him for the messiah. We were in need of salvation, you see. His coming gave us more room to commit misdeeds. And here came Bogomil with his glowing ears that sometimes doubled as wings. He landed on Earth complete with white robes, apocalyptic stories, trinkets of seashells, and the usual third eye. So we listened to the words he never uttered, wept in awe at the miracles he did not perform.

Bogomil's Ceremonial Stage: Caspar and His Props

after Otto Rapp's *Bogomil's Ceremonial Stage: Caspar and His Props*

(1983)

acrylic on canvas

14 × 10 in.

Caspar, Bogomil's sidekick, started the riot of prayer rallies and theater assemblage that featured exaggerated feats by Bogomil as he cavorted with young ladies from stage to stage. Our favorite effigy was the singular blackened one created in the likeness of the Rorschach test's first image. Yes, the one that was supposed to look like a butterfly, although most folks insisted it was a moth. Some comments in the guestbook passed around by Caspar described the thing as Icarus before or after his wings melted, a vagina, a phone book opened to entries starting with Z, a microwave oven with a poorly fitting door, an artichoke pickled in squid ink, etc. Each day, we convinced ourselves that its form had changed, its colors had shifted. The effigy followed us in our dreams. Each time we woke, we were certain we had pinpointed what it was.

Everything That Rises

after Julie Heffernan's *Self-Portrait as
Everything That Rises*
(2003)
oil on canvas
78 × 82 in.

And when the birds from hell burned down the cathedral that day, they understandably started with the chandelier. Nothing we did was good enough. No water in the world could douse the flames. The birds finally flew out of the church's steeple. They looked like ordinary birds, only that their wingtips were ruffled by the fire. By midafternoon, the cathedral was a mound of ashes and smoking rubble. It took us a year to rebuild, losing thirty-two men in the process. Two days later, the birds brought down the whole structure again. We spent another year putting the cathedral back together, stone by stone, one vaulted dome after another.

The very next day, we razed it with our bare hands, laughing and crying and daring the damned birds to stop us.

Self-Portrait as Broken Home

after Julie Heffernan's *Self-Portrait as Broken Home*

(2008)

oil on canvas

67 × 57 in.

What will the surgeon say if he opens us up only to find rooms of unfinished lives? What will he make of the unmade bed, the living room where a television set plays reruns of breakfast cereal commercials, the Christmas tree erected in the middle of July, those loose floorboards, the attic of cockroaches, toys, and discarded chandeliers, and the aquarium of venomous sea creatures? Will he understand our need to look tough, to look smarter than the rest? Or will he see through our weakness? And shaking his head in disgust, will the surgeon resist the impulse to peer in through the incision, thrust his hand into our bellies to diagnose bad plumbing, and wade through the muck of unpainted rooms and guts stringed to create space for guests? After all this, will he stitch us up in time, slap a *For Sale* sign on our bloody doors?

Self-Portrait as World

after Julie Heffernan's *Study for Self-Portrait as World*

(2008)

oil on canvas

40 × 46 1/2 in.

We sway on waterlogged feet, what's left of them anyway. We are this stout orb of free will and disappointment, building our houses to reach the upper hemisphere. This unstable world so landlocked it is impossible to explore what lies below, underneath the watery surface lapping at the globe's lower end. This lack of stability has kept us alive. Every day, we wait for that tiny shrug, for the minuscule wobble that will send us rolling downward.

Self-Portrait as Sky Scraper

after Julie Heffernan's *Self-Portrait as Sky Scraper*

(2008)

oil on canvas

68 × 60 in.

When we were told to outgrow our beginnings, we grew upward. Skyward. Each person a tower of stacked rooms. The transparent walls allowed us to view what was outside but never the room below.

Inside these rooms, we blew out birthday candles with ease; the lack of windows prevented the draft from entering. We slumped no longer at the dinner table. We cultivated sunlight and good manners with ornamental lamps. And what little light they offered, we extinguished with the slightest movement of our lips.

We kept the rooms tidy for there were no holes through which to discard useless things.

The gods of separation and boredom grinned at the mantel displaying the framed collages of birds. How we dusted them every day.

Outside, the whole world, a merry carnival of dead ends, roadblocks, dams, and flooded canals.

At the bottom of the deepest well, gravity called our name.

Self-Portrait as Big House

after Julie Heffernan's *Self-Portrait as Big House*

(2006 - 2007)

oil on canvas

68 × 58 in.

The red, electric posts will hold, and our lights will never go out. There's a fountain on our belly button. It draws water from a stagnant pool that grows inside our left knee. The water is clear now; the abscess has been removed. What remains is a scab of moldy skin surrounding the pool. Its putrid smell reaches far during the summer.

It does not matter if the lower torso is ugly and diseased. As long as the brain is a merry continent of carnival tricks and fetish rooms, as long as the only ladder carries us from one exposed room to another, as long as Matilda, the landlord's daughter, does not burn the attic down with her experiments in alchemy, the house will live on.

And a child inside the white airplane passing overhead will wave and smile at us.

Abandoned Dwellings

after Vladimir Kush's *Abandoned Dwellings*

What we always leave behind is an unrecorded catalogue of the things that went wrong. There's the depression of a window on the unpainted side of the house. There's that book filled with bluebirds, filled with woodchips, filled with nightmares, filled with burned-out lamp bulbs and mismatched socks. And if we have said something in the past, then we have said nothing at all. So trudging along, we bury the landscape underfoot. We move from one shell to the next, leaving by the side of the road a litter of colorful husks. We travel light, and everywhere we go, there's an entire universe of abandoned dwellings.

House and Men

after Vladimir Kush's *Wind*

When viewed from below, we are all versions of staircases at various angles. There's the one who carries the ladder. There's the figure burying the body in the backyard. There's the forlorn one, the smirking one, the one whose hands are filled with carpentry tools. The hired hands wear gloves when collecting garbage. On the front porch are the slats of a broken daughter we all wish we could hammer back down. The windows bend outward, expelling the wind. Guilt escapes in all the right places. A giant blue shirt billows where a roof should be.

Hope

after Jacek Yerka's *Little House on the Prairie*

acrylic on canvas

54 × 66 cm

Hope is a flatland where horses make hoof marks on dust. Or better yet, hope is a tiny wooden house with a yellow door. This house is small enough that nothing will fit inside; household items are kept outdoors. The sink, the stove, the kitchen implements, the phonograph—everything is strewn across the desert yard. This house's occupant has no choice but to sleep outside. Even in the absence of wind, a makeshift weathervane swings on the roof.

For the One Who Got Away

after Don Stewart's *Hiking Boot*

drawing

21 × 18 in.

Here's a handful of pebbles from the ravine into which I've accidentally fallen. Here are chunks of rock from the outcropping my busted left kneecap snagged. And here, here's the tuft of grass I was clutching. All this before I tore off my elbow joint while sliding, when I could have been doing something else, something that did not require broken bones. Recycling the same bag of trail mix for luck did not work. It was noontime at the peak of summer. The heat didn't bother me at all.

Bad Egg

after Max Ernst's *Oedipus Rex*

(1922)

oil on canvas

93 × 102 cm

That day, he had the optometrist cut his second eye out of the natural cracks in his calcium-enriched shell. After, he couldn't take his new eyes off the framed portrait of Humpty Dumpty on the optometrist's gilded mantel.

The image of Humpty Dumpty, glaring insolently from atop the brick wall as the king's men held their breath below, haunted him. It was everything he wanted to be. He had grown tired of his life—the staggering, the delicate white shell that enclosed and stifled his protein soul, his will.

One night, he told his little brother about his plan.

Crying, his little brother reminded him of the grisly omelet crimes on TV.

"They're gonna put you into one of those refrigerators. It's gonna be dark and cold and ugly!" the little brother said, his voice a squeal, his shell trembling with fear. It took great effort for him not to rattle his nerves and break.

"Then they'll crack you up and kill you!" the little brother screamed as a last, futile attempt to impart sense into his stubborn, egg-headed big brother.

But no one could scare the hell out of this bad egg; even an electric egg beater's gory instruction manual failed to discourage him.

By dawn, the bad egg had left the hole and, like other renegades before him, never came back.

Cactus Man

after Odilon Redon's *Cactus Man*

(1881)

charcoal

49 × 32.5 cm

You have to understand that the pot is designed to constrain your growth to just a few inches, the optimum size of man to be controlled. A man whose sole purpose is to grow thorns in order to collect nourishment cannot be left to his own devices. That springboard neck stunted by never looking down. That torso a barrelful of jack-in-the-box surprises. You would slither straight into our gullible hearts if you could.

Once a week, we water your sand. How your eyes blossom yellow for more.

The Spider

after Odilon Redon's *The Crying Spider*

(1881)

charcoal

49.5 × 37.5 cm

Your own family betrayed you the day they mistook you for a spider. Your mother caught you balancing a coffee mug on your fourth leg while sewing a button onto your coat with your two inborn hands. She told the family doctor you were "not quite right." Another day, spying through the half-opened door, your kid brother watched you spin a web on the bedroom ceiling. Turning around, your eyes locked with his. He screamed. You didn't get a chance to lick your achy joints and explain to him that it is normal to spin a web, to trap insects. Afterwards, your brother had to be sedated. For two years, he had the same bad dream. Your father, saddled since birth with pretending to be human, blamed you. When at last you had the sense to run away from home, nobody reported you missing. Your family must have assumed that anyone with eight legs must travel farther, go places no one else can. Most days, you wish that were the case.

Nowhere Room

after Mike Worrall's *The Never Ever Room*

(1998)

oil on panel

122 × 155 cm

Theophilus is wedged in the wooden floor of his temperature-regulated chamber called Childhood. Drawing moths during the summer, a 50-watt switch bulb dangles from the ceiling.

His mother says: "You only fill one small room when you die so there's no sense in occupying more while you are alive."

He nods, never talks back.

"A good parent can either teach you to forage or to be safe. I choose to keep you safe." Then she slams the door only to reappear at the end of the day with food.

Theophilus grows bigger, older. His limbs approximate those of a man's. His senses of smell and hearing grow acute.

Outside, the schoolchildren taunt him, throw stones at the window, and leer at him—the pale-skinned boy anchored since birth to the floor of his room. Theophilus will not admit it, but he covets the schoolchildren's teeth, ruined by too much candy and soda. He admires their unruly hair, which smells of summertime. He loves to hear them call him "ugly" because it makes him feel unique and important.

Each day, the windows and doors shrink a little. In time, even his finger will not fit.

Gregor Samsa Plays the Flute

after Peter Marcek's *Spev zeme*

Gregor Samsa, the giant worm, was growing uglier as we drew nearer, and his stench was becoming unbearable. So we concentrated on his music, the wordless whimpers of a creature that had no eyes, no feet, and no hands. His sister held the flute close to his mouth. It looked as if he was about to swallow the musical instrument, but he held off. He huffed and puffed like no other great worm could. We did not see the pustules on his back as a result of being bedridden. But the perforations on his body where black liquid trickled out were hard to miss. Gregor must have accidentally swallowed some twigs and sharp-edged indigestibles because some had pierced his belly. If he wasn't propped upright, we wouldn't have noticed that he still had a head. If he did not insist on finishing whatever melody he was trying to conjure off that slime-slicked flute, we would never have known he was dying.

The Misunderstood

after Man Ray's *The Misunderstood*

(1938)

Every creature cries in its own time. Except this one.

It assumed the shape of a leaf, a teardrop. It had a beak that doubled as a nose. It exposed its veins so we could see it had nothing to hide. It was bloodless, seemingly dead. A young princess once underestimated its loneliness, how far it would go to disguise itself as happy.

He might have started as a talking frog. A swarthy creature that had the sense to fetch the ungrateful princess's golden ball when it ended at the bottom of the well.

"Silly little thing," she said, as she accepted the ball he had dredged from a watery hell. "I am the king's daughter. Why should I let you sleep on my bed?"

Getting what she wanted, she left him croaking, pissed off, and ripped off like the frog he was. Undaunted, he hopped toward the castle. He swayed the king with rhetoric about "honoring one's promise," until he found himself sleeping on the princess's puffy pillow, kissing her as she slept, inserting his tongue into her mouth as she dreamt of having sex with her older sister's husband.

He never became human as it would have taken years for amphibious traits to be shed for mammalian ones. But he did learn to blend in. Sometimes, we plucked him off a stalk, confident that we could just sniff him; that the crackling sound had nothing to do with this paper-thin, leaflike, smiling thing.

The Seashell

after Odilon Redon's *Le coquillage*

(1912)

pastel on paper

57.8 × 52 cm

Whenever we turn you over to inspect your underside, you presume that we care. Strange how you don't require dismantling in order to confess the ocean trapped inside your folds. Once dead, you become an object of art washed up on the shore of this watery museum. And oh, what a pink smile you have.

The Adulterer

after Dorothea Tanning's *Interior with Sudden Joy*

(1951)

oil on canvas

24 × 35 3/4 in.

You always recognize the wild ones, the way they turn their heads as if they don't notice that you have been staring at the outlines of their breasts. Their names usually start with *S*, the hiss like a prelude to a long evening. You tell Irish jokes. You loosen your tie. You embrace the amorphous sculpture in the center of the room. The wild ones laugh. You think it shows you have no inhibitions, like a middle-aged man caught between common sense and plain old lust. You leave a book half-open on a purple velvet pillow. On the page is a riddle about desire. As you quote from it, your wife enters the room carrying a bounced check and a jar of your aborted child. Your ex-wife exits using the back door. She shields her face with her faux-alligator purse. She is not drunk and hasn't smoked in a very long time. She is trying to hide her smirk.

Man in a Black Suit

after Philippe Ramette's *Rational Exploration of the Undersea* photo series

Here is an average-looking hero who will hold his breath underwater long enough to read a map, take a nap, pose beside a rusty anchor nearly twice his size, name every shipwreck he encounters after the girls who broke his heart.

Each day, he falls in the wrong direction. Mostly upward. He then ascends downward, against the current. The blue waters always find him intact. Or is it the other way around? Sink or float, his black-suited form will appear larger than a lighthouse, larger than the rest of us put together.

Given the chance, he will touch the surface of the water. Balancing atop a collapsible ladder propped on the sea floor, he will make contact and broach the still surface. Out of the void, where his hand should be, he will beckon to the beautiful girl who lost the moon he once offered her.

Moon Sonata

after Sergey Laisk's *Moon Sonata*

(2009)

oil on canvas

130 × 63 cm

Did you see Ben on the precipice, the overhanging rock ledge leading to the moon? There was no god (or iterations thereof) when that geological anomaly was formed. Did you see him touch the surface of the moon? We weren't sure if it was only perspective, like the way the Leaning Tower of Pisa looks portable when viewed from a certain angle.

Ben had his hand outstretched as if proclaiming: "Here's this rounded and luminous arc of greatness. I may slip from this precarious position and die, but I touched the moon. Nothing else mattered."

Dryland

after William C. Tumley's 1990 photograph of the dried-up Aral Sea

The sun-bleached sands retained the impression of water currents. The bones of fish and long-extinct sea creatures crunched underfoot as we waded in sand that had once lain at the bottom of the sea. Exposed, we had nothing to offer but the picture of these grisly shipwrecks, the occupants of which were long gone. It had to happen at some point. Naturally, we were greedy, hard to please. It was easy to divert the water flow, siphon it to irrigate croplands. Until at last, we were left with this minor problem of towing the rusting shipwrecks, cargo ships and oil tanks, back to their nonexistent harbors. We can still salvage them for parts, you know, gut everything to the bone.

Strange how we shiver in the desert heat. If we breathe deeply enough, there's still the hint of a sea breeze. We were here once. As children, our feet tested the waves lapping at the shore. And not once have we wondered whether they were real.

The Collage Artist

after Otto Rapp's *Longing*

(1973)

acrylic on canvas

22 × 30 in.

They said she had a hand in all this. They said that, after he was introduced to her, he was never the same, wore that glazed look, like a puppy that didn't need a leash.

With her veiny hands, she scissored each red-paper cutout to fit the frame, adorned it with torn-up maps and split-ended strands of hair. She juxtaposed familiar objects with strange terrains. Patched-up lonely hearts on canvas, grattage on the right edge to simulate texture.

They said there was no way she could have charmed him with her matronly ways and pockmarked face. They said something did not seem right.

What little light he had left she scrunched in gold foil, affixed as light beams to the matted board above her stars.

Every night, she took out the bound doll, caressed the button eyes, and tightened the stitches against the stuffing, his nail clippings and locks of hair still inside the doll's stomach.

Birth of the Dream Monster

after René Magritte's *Elective Affinities*

(1933)

oil on canvas

41 × 33 cm

When René woke from a deep sleep, he discovered that the bird inside the cage had regressed into an egg. Assuming that it had been placed there intentionally, René was slow to realize that not all plain white things mean no harm. There were times when the egg swelled to nearly the size of the birdcage, although most days it remained small enough to go unnoticed. A silent white orb that couldn't gesture at anything. The bird never reappeared. It was either René dreamed it out of existence, or, by chance, it reverted back to its embryonic form. Either way, the circumstances were unsettling. Here was a creature that would betray its owner. Here was a pet that would replace its master. René should forever dread waking to discover the birdcage door swinging open.

Cow No. 7

after Wendy Detrick Worsham's *Cow Number 7
Wandered Off Again*

False walls keep the landscape replete with color-saturated rural scenery. This serene green a premonition: *something is about to go wrong*. Cow No. 7, the mutant one irradiated since birth with small doses of gamma rays, has just found a way to jump the electric fence. And there it is, wiggling its ears, pretending to be normal to gain acceptance from the other grazing cows. It acts dumb to be one of them: no eye contact, no attempts at communication except for the typical low-pitched *moo*, no bad-mouthing the fattest ones, the ones that are first to be butchered. We admire its determination to fit in and lead a normal cow's life. It may not have been too much to ask. Cow No. 7 even resisted the urge to tell us to go to hell when it was about to be collared and taken back to the institute.

Revenge of the Goldfish

after Sandra Skoglund's *Revenge of the Goldfish*

(1981)

It started when my sister and I painted the bedroom walls an incestuous blue. At first, only two appeared, *seeped* through the walls. *Goldfish.* All fat lips and yellow-orange ugliness, squiggling as if they had the right to materialize. One landed near my sock drawer. The bigger of the two settled on top of the blue lamp. The fish wheezed as they died, waiting for water. It got worse each day. In a week, goldfish poured from the ceiling, the unadorned walls, the dresser mirror, under the blue bed. Hundreds. Their husks dropped on the floor. Even in our sleep, we could hear their gasps. We trod on their bodies as we dressed for work, back to the world that did not know what we had to endure inside this little room. We only collected them when we could no longer stand the smell, that pungent, moldy odor of decay. We talked of moving out, although by the time there was gurgling in the bathroom pipes, we knew it was too late.

The Ugly

after Otto Rapp's *The Minotaur*

(1976)

acrylic on canvas

18 × 24 in.

Sewing shut your skull, split open by the apocalypse, brought you back to life. It was impossible to repair what was left. Your head, which was also your body, slowly inched out the door. A nose like a misshapen beak propped up the distorted rest of you. You sniffed as you squished across the floor, leaving a trail of snot and clotted blood. Beside your left ear was a forlorn horn, a grisly remnant from a previous life in which you were a mythical creature revered by men of magic. We sometimes mistook it for other things: a shard of skull, a hardened tongue, a club of some sort, a burnt stake that an incompetent exorcist forgot to remove. We had no common language, yet you understood our revulsion. Your sole functioning eye stared out at the gloom of this life in which you were the only one of your kind left living.

Birthday

after Dorothea Tanning's *Birthday*

(1942)

oil on canvas

102 × 65 cm

It only happens once a year, seventy times in an entire lifetime if you live to seventy. The first one starts with you breaking open a translucent bag of water. Your familiar, a winged, mouse-looking creature that scares easily, watches you sleep in your crib. Whenever you feel hurt or happy, it does, too. Every year, you open a white door leading to more white doors. The familiar, your dumb extension, follows you around, scampers after you as you inspect what lies behind each door. Every room is an empty room before you leave it. Your familiar does nothing but drop a hairball. Sometimes, fouling itself, it squats and deposits an inky thing in the corner of the room. Nearing middle age, you discover that you are a wild swan. So you wear a feathered skirt. You learn a clucking language. You even steal a costume too absurd to wear in public. At some point, you reach the last door.

The one that opens to the grim finality of a broom closet or an unused bathroom. For the first time, your familiar hesitates to follow. You think nothing much can happen inside a room this small. You expect it to be easier to fill than the others before it. But perhaps, this time, you are wrong.

Evening Ceremonies

after James Gleeson's *Evening Ceremonies*

(1986)

oil on canvas

175.5 × 265.7 cm

When you open your eyes for the first time after death, tell us what you see. Are there trees around? Vegetation? Are you in a desert dotted with red-blossomed cacti? There must be a ferry. Old Man Böcklin tells us this, and he speaks from experience. And if there is a boat, there is a body of water. Let's say the roiling mass underneath your boat is some sort of river. It must lead somewhere. Which way is heaven? North? How about hell?

How quickly should you paddle against this foul-smelling muck?

Since the laws of perspective are impermeable, you must perceive where the sky ends and the horizon begins. Does it seem like it's about to rain? When you look up, can you determine which blackened husk corresponds to the sun?

What Better Lure

after Giorgio de Chirico's *The Double Dream of Spring*

(1915)

oil on canvas

56.2 × 54.3 cm

A man in a gray suit watches his future unroll:

A desert sinkhole gobbles the red balloon he let go of as a child. A future wife embraces another man. He closes his eyes for two seconds so he doesn't see what they do with their tongues. Shadows flit about; sometimes he can tell that their stillness is the result of their moving too fast. A man turns his back on a building. A man stands before a building. A man misses the train. An empty water glass on a bedside table. His sickly form no longer on the bed, no longer refilling the water glass, no longer waiting for the phone to ring. And there in the middle is a framed architectural plan, the rough sketch of a wonderful life that remains unfinished.

Insomnias

after Dorothea Tanning's *Insomnias*

(1957)

oil on canvas

207 × 146 cm

They give birth to several extensions of themselves, each likeness farther apart, even when holding hands. This whole life a waking dream beckoning to them from the street below. A window slat opens every morning, finds them intact but with pooling blood underneath their heads. Even in death, they are wide-eyed.

Damocles

after Heidi Taillefer's *Damocles*

(2010)

oil on canvas

101.6 × 152.4 cm

He was irreparably bent and stunted from years of balancing the counterweight of the pulleys that run the factory. Once a year, he was permitted respite: a daylong break spent coupling with a girl named Repression who never once called him by name. He mistook every time she ignored him for love.

By midnight, he arrived at his usual spot near the charging station. His shoulders clamped with stainless steel manacles attached to metal chains. The turbines started. The generators chugged. The city was alive once again.

The Great Architect

after Salvador Dalí's *Surrealist Architecture*

(ca 1932)

He built a pyramid out of taffy, skylight windows out of egg whites. He constructed our houses to be soft to the touch. Everything bends to our weight and conforms to our needs. In the highways behind the only ossified savannah left in the world, rabbits are plastic. They pretend to freeze before headlights. They pretend to fear death. This alone inflicts a sense of normalcy.

Giorgio at the Piazza

after Giorgio de Chirico's *Piazza d'Italia*

(1913)

oil on canvas

35.2 × 25 cm

This is the story of a man who sleeps with his eyes open.

At the right time of day, when the sun casts a perpendicular shadow of the piazza, he stands at the self-appointed spot by the mausoleum. There, he meets himself, shakes hand with himself. Both men sizing up the other's likeness. Two separates, not halves of each other. This scene lasts two minutes, depending on the weather. Then perspective dissolves and there is only one man left standing by the mausoleum.

Farther to our right (his left), the steam locomotive accelerates, toward him in the background. When observed from this part of the courtyard, the vehicle looks as if it will slam into the stone tower. In his mind, he hears the sound of the crash. In his mind, there are no survivors.

This is a Headshot

after Edvard Munch's *Self-Portrait with Skeleton Arm*

(1895)

lithograph

45.5 × 31.7 cm

Here, in this painting they display in a museum in Norway, I try to look morose. It is dark. It always is. Like poet Jack Gilbert intuits as the "soft machinery of the dark." Soft because the dark is elastic, because you can make it last if you want. My black sheath lends an illusion of decapitation. My mustache offers me the air of an educated man; it helps when you cannibalize your self-portrait to buy your syphilitic ladylove something shiny. I show them my broken arm, straightened across the window ledge before me. The bone is exposed. It was an accident. Nobody will listen to my side of the story. It may look painful, but perhaps it isn't.

Colored Pencils

after Paulo Rosa's *coloured absynthesis - coloured pencils*

We hope our staunch, wooden chrysalis will someday let us out, eject us from your grasp. Sharpened, we grow blunter, methodical, like relics that have lost their will to be more than showroom objects. Our eyes bleed a thousand colors as you push us against paper. Funny how you think these strokes are yours. They are our pain, you see, our stories.

The Red Orchestra

after Salvador Dalí's *Music - The Red Orchestra -*
The Seven Arts
(1957)
oil on canvas
84 × 116 cm

We shaped ourselves into violins whenever we sought strumming. Into pianos, when we ached to be touched in places no one could reach. There were tubas and percussions, the shrunken and the bloated. We comfortably let out our breath in metered intervals, but most days we weren't in the position to breathe at all. The musicians pretended not to notice the blood welling from where our flesh tore apart as we twisted into familiar instruments. The bony fingers of the conductor coiled and uncoiled, slashed the air with the precision of a matador's sword striking bone. The audience sat in awe, entranced by the sound of our pain.

Sphinx Embedded in the Sand

after Salvador Dalí's *Remorse* or

Sphinx Embedded in the Sand

(1931)

oil on canvas

19.1 × 26.9 cm

They discovered one day that their daughter had grown into a giant sphinx. She was as tall as a thirty-storey building, and was buried from the waist down. The ossified city tried to pacify her to avoid earthquakes, but it was impossible to catch her attention. Her insufferable height prevented her from making out details on the ground below. "Where were you when I tore off my face?" she wailed. "I told you I cannot be let out of my room. I told you I cannot be like everyone else," she bellowed to the figures dressed in black coats. She thought they were her parents so she nagged, scolded, and blamed them for her misfortune. Watching television inside a ramshackle cabin three thousand miles away, her real mother and father cried when the black helicopters arrived, machine guns blazing.

Startled Emu

after John Olsen's *Startled Emus*

mixed media on paper

90 × 70 cm

The hunter crouched in the bushes. A cramp was starting to form in his left leg. When the shot rang out, the emu assumed it was the target. Being the center of attention meant being the first to die. It was the hereditary conditioning of prey. Panic caused its lopsidedness, a dainty stick figure with no ambition. It sprinted. It would never look back, would never, even for a second, turn to discover which of its companions lagged behind.

The Dour Elephant-Kettle

after Max Ernst's *Célèbes* or *The Elephant Célèbes*

(1921)

oil on canvas

125.4 × 107.9 cm

You worthless kettle, when will you hiss as you boil the Master's tea? Your bulbous form is taking over the kitchen stand, yet you fail to act like a household implement. I am a contraption, too, but I know my purpose; I am humbled by the fact that I cannot function without electricity. Since birth, your limp tusk attached to your umbilical cord. Nobody wants to tweak it out of sight. I would, if I had hands.

The Storyteller

after Jean-Marie Poumeyrol's *Le Lavoir*

(1977)

acrylic on wood

90 × 71 cm

Once upon a time, a boy chooses to become a spider, to learn how to build webs of spit in which to trap small insects. His pudgy torso remains suspended on the ceiling like the husk of Rumpelstiltskin, spindly legs stowed so as to look inconspicuous. This boy-spider grows up and goes into the world carrying burlap satchels filled with the insects he has captured. Every day, he offers strangers a bite. Some find the taste bitter. Some claim it is just right.

How the Invisible Man Gives Himself Away

after Salvador Dalí's *The Invisible Man*

(1932)

oil on canvas

140 × 81 cm

He steps on some toes and never looks back. When faced by the crowd, he keeps his head low. It doesn't matter if nobody notices his single act of humility. At nighttime, he screams inside his invisible shell.

There is only one window in his chamber, and it doesn't allow anything inside. Not even the light. He does not know where he is going with his life until the day he gets lost.

Obliterating the Outcast

after Yves Tanguy's *Mama, Papa is Wounded!*

(1927)

oil on canvas

92.1 × 73 cm

They drag you out of the cabin. The real wolfman snickers behind one of the windows, one of those boarded up to keep the weak from being hunted at night. The women who cast the first stones shiver around the candlelight, convincing everyone how sure they are of your guilt. What they know, what they were like before they came here, is out of the question. You manage to bite the man who ties you to the stake. Reduced to ashes before dawn, you probably never existed. Nobody remembers you. Not even that strange odor you emit.

Milk Maiden

after Beau White's *Milk Maiden*

oil on board

Had to wear a cow's head to keep up with the neighbor's beautiful wife. Had to chew cud, stand proudly on the grass. Had to let the little ones nip your breasts. Had to produce milk. Had to learn animal sounds. Had to swing your tail to keep the flies away from your behind. Had to be a lovely, lovely maiden with docile eyes.

A Much Younger Wife

after Max Ernst's *Woman, Old Man and Flower* or

Femme, viellard et fleur

(1923 - 1924)

oil on canvas

96.5 × 130.2 cm

This was where he discovered her, crouched among the discarded mattresses and standing lamps. She looked away to hide her dirty face when he reached out to touch her left cheek. Her fingernails were ragged, chewed to stubs. He squeezed her left arm and led her to his idling car. Another old man opened a passenger door not far from them. It was early summer, and the search for new wives was in full swing.

The Perilous Compassion of the Honey Queen

after Carrie Ann Baade's *The Perilous Compassion of the Honey Queen*
(2009)
oil on panel
18 × 24 in.

I brought him the nectar of a thousand flowers. I didn't have to, but I did. When you drown someone you love, you have to do it right. So I drew him a bath, lulled him to sleep. In his dreams, the bees never tire because they are busy dying for their queen. Chartreuse and gold honey oozes from my mouth and from the slashes on my wrists. A trickle first, then a gush.

His son found him two days later. Crushed dandelions and calla lilies were crammed down his throat. With his face contorted like that, nobody could tell he had been loved.

Dangerous Liaisons

after René Magritte's *Dangerous Liaisons*

(1926)

oil on canvas

72 × 64 cm

She was set up with a mirror. When he (the mirror) looks at her, she sees herself. Unclothed. Her bare-assed odalisque. As if shielding her breasts. Turning away slightly as if holding something back.

The Couple in Lace

after Max Ernst's *The Couple* or *The Couple in Lace*

(1925)

oil on canvas

101.5 × 142 cm

Even your motives are transparent, your sarcasms laughable. Your lace-wife opens her legs; we hear smut and tackiness. The antics of a tablecloth runner are impossible to take seriously. You smack your lips to incite a laugh, and we hear the crackle of dry fabric, the rumble of wind through your perforated skin.

René Magritte, the White Cloth, and the Lovers

after René Magritte's *The Lovers*

(1928)

oil on canvas

54 × 73 cm

If only they did it with a bit of decency, they wouldn't have kissed while their heads were swathed in opaque white cloth. What was anonymity but the reluctance to engage in foreplay at the front doorway? He was in a dark suit, a plain black tie, probably works uptown in a bank or law firm, probably married. Or he could have been a secret agent, some sort of spy. Real women, in general, love the dangerous ones, the reckless ones, the famous poseurs who die young (typically at twenty-seven) after blowing off their heads with shotguns.

Only this scene is not real. She was a spinster, had halitosis. They were not actually kissing. He was there to serve a foreclosure notice. She was trying to look over his shoulder. The upstairs neighbor slung a makeshift clothesline on the terrace above them. The white cloth, loosened by the wind, drifted over their heads at the right moment.

Birdcage

after Nicoletta Ceccoli's *Birdcage*

We could have mistaken for love the way he looked at you—you, the half-maiden, half-parrot perched on the brass pedestal once used for a bridal showcase. Two light bulbs burned out during the course of your interrogation. The birdman was uncomfortable in his chair. He never shifted. You would have detected his weakness. He did not hide the wires and electrodes used to measure your fear. Expressionless, you stared back and chirped no more.

Bad Love and Carnage

after Joel-Peter Witkin's *Myself as a Dead Clown*

(2007)

silver print photograph

190.5 × 190.5 cm

When she told the police what had happened, she swore to the presence of a black-winged intruder, a six-foot tall monstrosity with green eyes. Through smeared lipstick and morning breath, she recounted how her lover was assaulted: "It pecked at him as if he were a rag doll. That's why his chest was torn open, his ribcage exposed." She averted her gaze. There was a particular glint in her eyes that almost blurted: *Like a wasted clown smeared with red paint. He would no longer dance, the bastard.*

Again, she described the creature as a giant black bird. She produced an onyx feather the size of her outstretched hand to prove it. "A gryphon?" somebody joked. Sgt. Johnson from Homicide, his forehead furrowed, channeled the look of a man who recognized a gryphon.

The girl who took out the trash finally explained to him all there was to know about the mythical bird.

We took turns questioning her. Good cop/bad cop. The way they do it in the movies. She stuck to her story. *Once there was a gryphon that pecked to death a man inside a motel room that charges by the hour. The man's upper torso was mangled beyond recognition. There was also a soft-spoken lady that emerged from the ordeal unscathed.*

Inevitably, the case was dismissed. She spent six months in an institution, was released, married one of the psychiatric ward attendants, the wiry one with bad teeth.

Sgt. Johnson spent eleven years searching for the gryphon. No one in the department had the heart to stop him.

The Village of the Mermaids

after Paul Delvaux's *The Village of the Mermaids*

(1942)

oil on panel

104.3 × 124.1 cm

The golden-haired girls of this village do not blink. Their stoic gazes can be mistaken for either stubbornness or guilt. They sit at their doorways. Hands folded on their laps like repentant whores. Full-length skirts concealing either their lack of desire to bear children or their amputated legs.

Nobody comes to this town except an occasional salesman, the man in black peddling the wares of youth and eternal life in a bottle. The girls wait on their doorsteps for that salesman. They linger wearing their mother's perfume and pensive stare, rehearsed over years for lack of anything better to do.

One of them sometimes forgets to turn off the stove. One is hiding a body under the floorboards. One of them is indecisive regarding her will to die. One is blind and faking a vacant stare.

Self-Portrait as Netherworld

after Julie Heffernan's *Self-Portrait as Netherworld*

(2004)

oil on canvas

60 × 52 in.

She has been suspended from the ceiling long enough that she has turned into a chandelier. She tinkles light bulbs where once she had skin, evoking an atmosphere devoid of meaning. If this were isolation, then it was surely contrived. She wears her trinkets of yellow on her head, on her shoulders, on the upside-down folds of her bloodied skirt.

There's a puddle on the floor underneath her. The liquid catches fire in the daylight. Flames walk across this tiny swath of water when sunlight hits it squarely in the middle.

The white birds circle, waiting for worms to drop onto the floor. Sadly, worms do not grow on chandeliers. But given the right conditions, she can transform into a birdbath.

Self-Portrait as Roots

after Julie Heffernan's *Self-Portrait as Roots*

(2009)

oil on canvas

72 × 56 in.

The little elephants underfoot scramble for cover. Her shifting weight has driven them from this world. They burst when stepped on. All this trampling and shuffling has revealed her roots. They clump to resemble, from the waist down, a trailing ball skirt. Sometimes, these exposed roots bear strange-looking fruit. Sometimes, she wills herself to eat them. Whatever she grazes on withers away, but something always survives in place of what doesn't.

Self-Portrait as Fiery Skirt

after Julie Heffernan's *Self-Portrait as Fiery Skirt*

(2008)

oil on canvas

60 × 52 in.

The combustible ones are beautiful yet usually don't last very long. Like this semblance of a girl who will not let anyone touch her. There she is by the lake, her upper body catching fire. She has plenty of time to jump into the water, but she chooses not to be bogged down by petty intricacies. The hem of her golden taffeta skirt laps at the water. She is laughing. She flails her arms wildly as if signaling for help, but the motion is only intended to fan the flames. The apple trees in the distance droop with the heat. Some of the fruit has ripened in the process. The whole world beyond this scenic lakeside, a ghost town.

Sketch for a Dirty Princess

after Julie Heffernan's *Sketch for Self-Portrait as Dirty Princess*

(2006)

6 1/2 × 6 1/4 in.

When the butler found the princess in the antechamber, she had already mangled most of the offerings to the king: the pheasant, the hog, the hare. All the swans, their necks violently twisted. Something that looked human was trampled beneath her petticoat. The butler was a sensible man; he did not look closely to see for himself the casualty.

At some point, rumors in the castle swirled about her poisoning one of the servants but not managing to kill her. She could have been honing her skills. None of us knew her motivations. It would have driven us all mad just to get close to understanding her.

"She's doing it because she can," Pascale, one of the guards, said.

We tried not to think of it this way.

The queen took a fatal fall down the stairs. A week later, the king died in his sleep. Her brother, Andrew, the next in line, left the castle after his coronation. He made a silly excuse about the immediacy of conquering a city south of Sicily that nobody, even the cartographers, had heard of. When the young king gave his final instructions to the chambermaids the morning of his departure, we sensed what he could never articulate: his unfounded fear of his fourteen-year-old sister.

Each day, her skirt of carnage grew. She left in her wake a smell of putrefaction. How we tried not to wrinkle our noses.

Each night, we left the candles to burn. We ignored the muffled screams of the tortured ones inside her closet, washed off the blood from the chopping block and knives she kept near her dresser.

Whenever she thought that somebody was spying on her, she hitched her skirt. And out would plop a severed finger or an eyeball.

For years, we bowed our heads in her presence. For years, we didn't look her in the eye.

For years, she wore her road kill and contraband of carcasses on her skirt.

The First Days of Spring

after Salvador Dalí's *The First Days of Spring*

(1929)

oil and collage on panel

50.2 × 65.1 in.

The first days of spring are always the toughest. Little girls learn to approach strangers near the monument for the patron saint of chickens. Dead bodies grow out of cracks on the roadside concrete; bankers harvest them before they sprout legs. A picture of a missing boy appears on the same fault line that splits the world in half, the upper crust of the Earth. The missing boy's father sits somewhere in an armless chair. The house where the chair was is no longer there.

In a week, everyone will get the hang of it. By then the elements of spring congeal at some sort of dead end, locking things in place, and there is normalcy. Fish wiggle out of a vase of tulips. A drunk and his transvestite companion discover a gold bucket filled with salt. A man uses his wife as a bicycle once more.

Bug Chairs

after Kazuhiko Nakamura's *Bug Chair*
3-D mechanical portrait

Before the girls were fashioned into chairs, their heads were severed by mechanical shears. The neck bones were sliced cleanly; their grins were locked in place, vacuum-packed and ready to ship. The upper torsos were irradiated and sent to taxidermists. Below the waist, parts were hammered down to serve as backs to armless chairs. The genitalia fully exposed. The legs wide-open in a *V*.

One Story About Flight

after Kazuhiko Nakamura's *The End of Flight Zone*
3-D mechanical portrait

Would you offer a yellow flower to court a girl who could fly? Night or day, her sonar eyes could probably detect your pathetic form waving at her from the ground, beckoning for her to stay low. Her rotor head buzzing, drowning out every sound. You would not be able to make out whether she said yes or no.

Rivalerne and Shelving

after Georg Broe's *Rivalerne*

(1968)

We do not know what they are, yet still they insist that they are just beautiful girls having their time in the sun. When girls evolve into wooden cupboards with long legs and perfect breasts, this is not the time to complain. So we let these girls be. Their wooden torsos creak when they walk, crack along the grain when they race to catch the train. They do not ride elevators. All the stairs and ladders in the world bend under their weight. Sometimes, they catch fire and are beyond help. Sometimes, their salvageable contents spill before the flames can reach them. As we watch them die, we imagine rearranging their tangled red hair, putting something on their empty, slowly burning shelves, inhaling the sawdust of their last breaths.

Surgical Addiction

after Gina Litherland's *Queen of an Uncharted Territory*

(2008)

oil on masonite

10 × 20 in.

Aunt Mimi is a waterless birdbath, a curvature in the middle of the yard that refuses to collect water. I watch her change shape twice, thrice a year, and don colors that indicate happiness. Her lips go from thin to full and back again. So do her cheeks, chiseled like those of a Greek vase's goddess. Her rump is a pillow where morsels of the dead are stuffed, stitched tight to keep out the foul smell. Her breasts are to the point of bursting through her blouse. They have evolved from conical to spheroidal, and when days are hot, they swell from dimpled limacons to cardioids—the whole chapter of mathematical curves I've learned in college. Her flat tummy, which I've thankfully never seen, was operated on by a doctor in Taiwan. It is bungled, resembling an ostrich skin with a basilisk's ridges.

Aunt Mimi admits to dreaming constantly about talking animals and how they mispronounce certain words to delude her. She even complains about the kitchen appliances breaking down one at a time. "Girl, there's no loss worse than the one you have," she says with certainty. Perhaps to emphasize her unlined forehead, she shields her eyes with her hand when she talks about sorrow, how old age is a nightmare that will not show its face, how it looms just a scalpel's breath away, killing her with anticipation.

Here's a B-movie pretending to be the last important square on the toilet paper roll. Here's the onslaught of winter doldrums gathering strength as they age.

And there's Aunt Mimi.

A True Story

after Dorothea Tanning's *Eine Kleine Nachtmusik*

(1943)

oil on canvas

16 1/8 × 24 in.

My girls had been tending the giant sunflower that sprouted on the hallway carpet at the top of the stairs. I told them to stop bringing it food, to starve it a little so that it wouldn't grow. It was not enough for them to know that the plant's being there was already a miracle. They could not be sated by doing no harm. One night, I caught them offering it sustenance. They confessed to experimenting first on the sunflower's appetite.

"It ate just about everything, Mother," they said.

I didn't make much of the strange gleam in their eyes.

And yes, the damned sunflower did eat everything. A goldfish, dog biscuits, dry cereal flakes, a coin purse, bits of bone, sequins, the hamsters. Things got out of hand when the girls disliked the Mississippi drawl of my chain-smoking third husband. They lured him into it. I had no choice but to make it look like an accident. The neighbors whispered, but that was all they could do.

I never admitted it to anyone, but I kept double-locks on my door from that time on. A mother should always preempt what might happen when her kids run out of things to feed a carnivorous sunflower.

Nobody's Beast

after Paul Booth's *Defiance*

oil on textured board

24 × 48 in.

When Jenna found the sleeping child inside the Kellog's box, its pink form was as big as her outstretched palm. This child-thing, she later discovered, was different from the others she had collected. Most of them died within the day. This child could be the one. It did not cry or ask for milk. But after a day or two, whenever it felt an itch or grew hungry, Jenna began to feel the same thing. She fed it just enough raisins and corn kernels that it would grow slowly enough not to seek any nurturing she was not accustomed to provide.

She stored the child in an old litter box she found under the sink, the one used for her first pet, Ducky, the irradiated dog with two tails.

The first few days were the hardest, as for any new mother. Whenever the child-thing stirred in its sleep,

Jenna felt restless. At the office, she messed up the spreadsheets so badly she had to rebuild everything from scratch.

It was a small price to pay for keeping a child.

When the child-thing was one, it grew to the size of Jenna's outstretched palms placed side by side. It had the features of a normal toddler, only much, much smaller. There were times when it would wake in the middle of the night and crawl toward Jenna's belly. This was the natural tendency of cereal-box babies as outlined on the cardboard back. They were not born the usual way so they were attracted to the womb. Swatting it away, Jenna heard the creature whimper as it curled into a fetal position at the bottom of the bed.

She could have thrown it away the first day. *Eat the cereal and discard the prize.* That was what most people did. Nobody wanted a kid whose ears would fall off. Nobody wanted a kid who would not cry. Now it was already too late.

It took her two more years to find the right father for the diminutive child-thing. Needless to say, the tiny man came from another cereal box.

The Taxidermist and the Girls Made of Dead Things

after Thomas Häfner's *Masken in zerfallener Umgebung*

(1974)

oil on canvas

59 × 49 cm

Something grew from the bruises and open wounds on their skin. Something with hands and eyes and a tongue and swollen lips. Something that would not complain when subjected to pain. Could not be killed by sharp objects or radiation. Something that would not break free.

The girls scratched and clawed themselves, conveying red across the room.

The taxidermist gave them a hand, excising whatever could be severed with a scalpel, leaving their backsides untouched and the hairballs inside their stomachs intact.

In time, the taxidermist built an empire of what he had managed to snip from the girls made of dead things. This empire was called Valentino or Gucci or something Italian-sounding. He fashioned leather purses and sold them at extravagant prices. The girls, in turn, slung his creations over their shoulders.

Industrial Farm Family

after Georg Scholz's *Industrial Farm Family*

(1920)

After the harvest, the industrial farm family had amassed so much money it became impossible to hide it all under the mattress. So the father punched a hole in his skull and stashed some there. The son had to help him force the blood-slicked bills inside. When space in the father's head finally ran out, the son was lobotomized to provide more storage room. This desperate act robbed the son of what little brain matter he had left. He grew into a village idiot who chased toads all his life, torturing the poor amphibians as he wished them into princesses for his soon-to-be harem.

Outside the house, the fat colonel was calling for help when the hem of his coat got caught in the blades of the grain thresher. He died a messy death. The family had to destroy part of the harvest because of the blood and guts.

The farmer's wife bought a golden hog and made it fat, fatter than the wealthiest man in Arkansas. During dinnertime, the father quoted verses from the family Bible. Only the golden hog listened to him drone on about the strange horses of the apocalypse.

The Half-Mermaid

after Georg Scholz's *Seated Nude with Plaster Bust*
(1927)

The half-mermaid would not budge unless she smelled water nearby. A long time ago, when the oceans still existed, she drifted away when forced to swim. She breathed in eddies and exhaled moss. As she grew older and was ultimately landlocked, we gave her enough time to daydream about her past life.

In art class, we worshipped her as she posed beside the plaster bust sculpted in her likeness. Her breasts were drooping. She crossed her legs to conceal the area where her finned tail had started to disappear.

Flowers, Secrets

after Nathan Spoor's *Promise*

(2005)

acrylic on canvas

40 × 32 in.

Home is always the most inappropriate place to begin one's life. There is only history there, and history cannot change anything. So on the day the second last of the Conners died, Marion Conner tended a flower garden in the front yard of the family's ancestral home.

This was the flowerbed where all her secrets grew names.

I don't know, Mother. It's Joanna. She did it! I tried to transform him, but his hands kept sinking back to his body....I know why my sister did it, Mother. She did it because it amused her.

There were dahlias, chrysanthemums, begonias, irises, and daisies planted in rows around a patch of ornamentals and smelly herbs. Perennials thrived in clusters behind the white fence.

Tell me, Bill, is it Anna? Don't lie. I can see it in your eyes. No one can deceive a Conner woman.

There were faces amongst the petals she did not want to see. One of them was Bill's. The first husband. He was pleading, his voice hoarse.

Marion recognized Martha Deidre's facial impression on one of the hydrangeas. Martha, a thin-lipped and voluptuous woman who had gossiped about Marion's family in the office, was shrieking in a tinny voice. The words were unintelligible. She had spread rumors long enough to be permitted to earn back her voice.

You see now, Marion? A Conner can only forgive but not undo. Once the words are out, you can never take them back. A spell is unbreakable, so much like the darkest of magic. Evil is something you cannot control.

Not this.

The garden was an empty tomb. Marion watched three bees gather. The very nature of bees is to seek and follow the trail of scents.

The drone of Bill's voice was lost to the buzzing of insects, the rattling of the wind. His other woman, Anna, was the face on the sole sunflower Marion had planted. Marion wanted the sunflower seeds to hurt Anna's eyes, to keep them closed most days so she would not have to meet her gaze.

Marion knew that they had suffered long enough for their sins, yet it was impossible for her to undo their fates.

I promise not to hurt. Promise, promise, promise....I'll never marry, Mother. I'll be alone the rest of my life. I don't want to hurt people anymore.

Marion tried to drown the screaming flowers with a sprinkler's water.

Rain of Men

after René Magritte's *Golconde*

(1953)

oil on canvas

81 × 100 cm

It poured men that day. From afar, they looked the same, although some had mustaches. Or cigars in their mouths. Or even stained teeth. It is difficult to tell when one is confronted with renderings of so many men with blackened mouths. Falling from the darkest of clouds like no other rain, they otherwise drifted down. Right-side up. Like the Mayan figures with oversized heads; everybody knew where the bases should be. Some had their hands inside their pockets. Their trench coats did not even flap. Bowler hats in place. When they touched down, the women tried hard not to inspect them.

The Ladders

after Georg Broe's *The Ladders*

(1968)

Some ladders are suspended in midair and remain parallel to the ground. These ladders are not meant to be mounted for there is no point in climbing a flat surface. Some ladders resemble trees, sprouting leaves to avoid detection. Some ladders are just ladders. Some ladders make themselves appear unstable to discourage potential climbers. Some ladders weep at the weight of our bodies, the slowness of our ascent. After we have climbed all two-hundred-and-forty rungs, some ladders bend so we end up where we started.

Some Roses and Their Phantoms

after Dorothea Tanning's *Some Roses and Their Phantoms*

(1952)

oil on canvas

76.3 × 101.5 cm

Some roses are scrunched balls of foil. They hop from one tabletop to another, glaring at toilet paper roses. Some roses, unless they huddle with others in a bouquet, do not believe they are roses. Some roses disguise themselves as roses; they want to be misunderstood. Some roses covet what other flowers have. Some roses wither as soon as you say their name.

People from the Drop of Water

after Jaroslaw Kukowski's *People from the Drop of Water*

oil

100 × 80 cm

They steady their unsteady forms by holding on to one another. Each watery glob grows the likeness of a head, the normalcy of a pair of limbs. Nobody wants to admit that they are made of water which is very common and very inexpensive. They spend their whole lives waiting for the moment when they can no longer keep their legs from dripping onto the ground. When they fall, it is either with a splash or a splat.

Time Transfixed

after René Magritte's *La Durée poignardée*

(1938)

oil on canvas

146 × 97 cm

The Master had it all wrong. When he set the clock, the hour hand was ticking to something other than time. We were shaking our heads when the locomotive emerged from the fireplace's brick wall. There was nothing we could do. Little by little, we turned into railroads to accommodate the oncoming train.

The Walking Lesson

after Jacek Yerka's *The walking lesson*

acrylic on canvas

54 × 65.5 cm

Time was a furry mammal with a dumb clock face. It took nine years to learn to use its emaciated legs. Its shrill breath fogged its glass faceplate. By accident, it sneezed and spat tiny chattering clocks of its likeness. The little clocks, their digital readouts and colored plastic coats, followed it around. Time had no sense of direction. Its merry brood skittered at its heels, unaware they were all going around in circles. Its tail stretched for miles, and chances were we had no clue we had been stepping on it once a day.

Bathyscaphe

after Jacek Yerka's *Bathyscaphe*

acrylic on canvas

54 × 54.5 cm

We dream of fish that are invisible and can never be caught. We dream of seas, too. Waters too perilous to allow the invisible fish to exist.

Underneath

after Jacek Yerka's *S.A.D.*

acrylic on canvas

54 × 61 cm

It does not make any sense given all the geology lessons we've attended, but there's a world underneath the ground where the leafless trees bear apples. We discovered it one April morning. We were searching for water, our dowsing rods poking every telltale patch of land.

Believe it or not, what lies six feet below is hollow. Barren trees prop up the ground. The branches are strong enough to carry the weight of the world, the weight of our disbelief.

We make a hole just large enough to pass a bucket through. Well water springs from where the roof of hell begins. We lower the bucket to scoop out water. Understandably, it is warmer than the usual tap.

The City is Landing

after Jacek Yerka's *The city is landing*

acrylic on canvas

54 × 62 cm

We do not travel on spacecraft. We arrive in hordes on the back of a dead planet. We carve out the entire city, entire villages and their inhabitants, then send them into space. The drawbridge we tuck out of sight to discourage marauders.

We land with a thud in the middle of what looks like marshland. The impact has decimated our tail, the unreinforced buildings where the commoners live. The castle and the courtyard are safe in the middle, and all our scientists have survived.

The air is thin but breathable. The gravitational pull makes movement more sluggish than we are accustomed to back home. Nice to see that on this particular planet acid rain hasn't managed to kill most of the trees. Strange how the branches bend even in the absence of wind. It is only days later that we realize these are not trees.

Attack at Dawn

after Jacek Yerka's *Attack at dawn*

acrylic on canvas

54 × 61 cm

When the patrol planes finally found the creature, it had already consumed its repast. Its once-bulbous body now assumed the shape of a Volkswagen Beetle. Door slightly ajar, it thumbed the remains of its meal: the edge of a chassis, the hard back of a rearview mirror, a portion of the steering wheel. Inch by inch, its reptilian tail contracted to form an exhaust pipe. It burped and spat out a license plate.

Prefab

after Jean-Marie Poumeyrol's *Le Blockhaus*
(1976)

And there it is, the familiar house of nightmares, trapped inside your mind. You try to look away from your impossible vantage point near the butcher's sink. Notice the strange cutaway of a house and how all its angles seem wrong. The walls are lightened by a hint of darkness. There are no people on the streets; everybody is in the house. They are inside learning their tap dance of isolation, the steps becoming more predictable. The music is only in their heads. You must keep your distance. Don't read between the lines. It is just a house. *Or is it?* At some point, you wake on the same bed. One incisor less.

City of the Dead

after Rick Hutchinson's *The Out of Towners*

acrylic on panel

Some of them were angry. Some had dirt under their fingernails, had mouths that puffed cigarettes like ticket dispensers—reckless yet methodical. Some of them were sure they would someday die painful deaths, hacking bloody phlegm. They knew it, and they smiled through yellowing teeth and diseased gums. Some smiled back, taking care not to shake hands. Some of them bloomed the marvelous heads of red poppies. Some laughed loudly in phone booths. The laughter sounded unforced. There was nobody on the other end of the line. Five minutes before punch time, some of them howled as they filled the elevators. Some took the stairs. Some jumped off the roof. Some poured coffee, skipped the cream. Some of them gathered around the water-cooler shrine, reveling in the intimacy of gossip and office talk. Some of them encountered the otherworldly inhabitants of skyscrapers. Could be the ghosts of long-dead construction workers. Could be anyone. Some clicked numbers and letters on keyboards that would soon translate into currency. The hum of centralized air conditioners and the muffled thumping of shoe bottoms on carpeted floors were the only normal sounds in the universe. Some of them just let time pass. Some knew where they wanted to go. Some did not want to get there. Some did.

In the lobby, the fat radio on the reception desk hums again about the end of the world, and some of them sing along.

Inside the Calorimeter Cup

after Max Ernst's *Castor and Pollution*

(1923)

oil on canvas

73 × 100 cm

We huddle with the other elements inside a controlled environment. This guy, Bill, will not stop licking his finger. Now his finger pad is bruised, and soon his blood will contaminate the broth. I hope they fish him out, recycle him with the other misanthropes, the maladaptives who cannot stop chewing gum, cannot stop whistling at the nude bodies fermenting on the floor.

A lab tech has left the vessel cover open to allow us to simmer, even gawk at the artificial landscape and its sky propped up around us. I hear the slurp of Bill's tongue around his finger, the melting degenerates' lewd comments as they graze the tank walls.

God, I hope I get to die sometime soon, get thrown with the castoffs into jars of chemical waste. How quiet it is inside those tinted jars. There's nothing like the absence of the mechanical stirrer, the terrible metal rod at the center of our world that prevents us from sinking. Its whirring sound has kept us awake for six years.

As Long As You Burn

after Karl Persson's *Dawn*

(2007)

oil on canvas

75 × 100 cm

The nuns in black, they cast no shadows. We waited for them to turn the corner and disappear. We could not imagine how many forms they took before they arrived. The least we could do was pretend they were invisible.

Come to think of it, it took us several lifetimes to conjure the finest end-of-the-world scenarios. Each to his own hell, after all. As long as you burn, no one can see through the wall of flames around you.

Inside a bedroom somewhere on Fifth Street, a doll-wife gyrated and stripped her clothes before the next husband.

Another man inflated one of those rubber Rapunzels, the kind that looked like our broken daughters.

Once again, the elusive juggernaut that walked on all fours squatted over Central Park, fouled itself with a hundred more spiders. We hunted those spider-creatures as a food source since we had to make do with what was left of the world. There were mushrooms, too, but we couldn't keep them down.

Somebody tried to build a house. The house replaced that person.

Somebody tried to plant sunflowers. The sunflowers did not exist.

Using a collapsible ladder, somebody was crazy enough to escape this makeshift world. He added one rung at a time. There was a void overhead where a good sky should have been. There was supposed to be a small door leading to a less depraved circle of hell. Each time the man almost touched the portal's metal handle, it moved an arm-stretch farther to his right. He had to shift the ladder once again, and from the ground upward to that distant door, construct it a rung at a time.

Boy with a Propeller Head

after Murat Turan's *Inception*

You probably started at dawn. You cranked the shaft attached to the propeller blades, waited for the engine inside your head to warm up, and went into the world.

Soaring, you realized it did not matter if you didn't look like everyone else, with those propeller blades sticking out from where your eyes and ears should have been. To us, you would have been ugly, a mechanical monstrosity; yet you could feel the wind over the woods, you could hear the ocean and the sloshing of the great fishes within. Your arms were free to touch the rustling branches of treetops, the tips of smokestacks and church steeples. You were even higher than the highest mountain peaks, although only for a while because the air was thin. No boy in the world could get so far. That made all the difference.

Some nights, you surely thought about what they would have said before you left: *When the wind stops churning and the propeller motor fails, where will you go, little boy? Will the journey be worth it?*

The foragers discovered your body near the creek bed. A squirrel nuzzled your foot, and a toad had found its way into your open mouth. The contraption you had welded onto your head until it grew into a full-blown propeller was a tangle of crushed metal and skull fragments. Even your parents found you unrecognizable. They said it could be any boy who had played a prank that went wrong. It could be any boy who had the nerve to fly away from home.

Tin Man Gets His Heart

after Sergio Rebolledo's *Warm*

Nobody wants a boy who will not squirm with this type of self-inflicted pain. Nobody wants a boy who doesn't allow himself to be broken, who trusts his parents to abandon him only because he thinks he is ready to be let out of his cage. When his elders instructed him to pick the chicken bones clean once he'd lifted them off the plate, it did not mean they wanted him to be healthy.

My little tin man, now fully grown yet half as precious as an unlabelled box. He still believes survival is a red umbrella that loses its owner in the middle of a storm. His portion of America is being spat on by baton-twirling girls who would have broken his heart, the heart with a snug fit inside his metal chest. Because we find him in this city, it means he is lost. And because he is wounded, he must have learned something.

Requiem for Industry

after Kazuhiko Nakamura's *Requiem for Industry*

(2007)

3-D mechanical portrait

When you did not come home one day, we knew they had chosen you to be fed to the machine, that contraption we once thought could save us from hunger. They must have selected you on the basis of height. We told you to hunch a little, slump a bit so that you would not tower over the rest.

We did not do a good job of raising you. We should have forced you to slouch to avoid being singled out. Your father blamed himself. I noticed him paying attention to the family revolver. For days, we waited for him to pull the trigger.

After they lugged you to the assembly line, they must have measured your sincerity with their metallic scopes. We had heard stories about torture involving water and electricity.

And since you had no information, what purpose did your severed limbs serve but to test the structural integrity of the giant mechanical maw. Bone chips to sharpen the blades. Your screams long lost to the thump of the suction pumps, the hiss of the steam valves. The conveyor belt carried away the rest of you, its chugging sound audible for miles.

Shadow of a Boy

after Otto Rapp's *The Visitor*

(1994)

acrylic on masonite

24 × 48 in.

Arthur opened one of the FedEx envelopes on the mantel and inspected its contents. Pictures and a medical certificate of a boy named Kelvin White slid out. He remembered the name from the local newspaper article he had read two days before. The boy had died after being hit by a stray bullet when two neighboring gangs went at each other.

He'd promised the boy's mother that he would have everything ready after Kelvin White's service. He would need to start working on the hands and feet that afternoon.

In the kitchen, one of the prototypes was making breakfast. Oppenheimer, the dog, nuzzled at its feet, impatiently asking for food.

"I'll take care of that," Arthur called. "Stay away from the stove." The heat could affect its hearing, a design flaw he had corrected in the new models.

"Yes, Arthur." It smiled and walked away after placing two golden pancakes on a plate. "I apologize for being a bother."

Arthur sometimes wondered what the boy-contraption with fake eyes could see, what it thought of him, its creator. Sure enough, it had the likeness of a boy aged about ten or eleven, but the glass eyes that Arthur bought from the taxidermist downtown looked artificial—pupils that would never dilate, irises that could not convey emotion.

Would this thing know pain? Would it know how to forgive or be happy?

Arthur wanted it to be safe. He had sent out too many, peopled the world with little boys and girls who would never grow up, would never hurt anyone or cause anyone to grieve. These machines—they would never get sick or feel ashamed or die.

Arthur was still trying to remember its name. All the early prototypes had looked alike, and all featured the same glass eyes. Before he was able to utter a sound, the creature approached him and politely asked for permission to leave the house.

The honk of the school bus beckoned.

The Apartment Building Before It Was Torn Down

after Sali Herman's *La ronde*

(1969)

oil on canvas

70.5 × 105.5 cm

The apartment building, a listless behemoth with painted-on brick façade, will sway on its foundation, yet will not fall. As children, we hold hands and sing around the puddle on the cracked pavement. We have mistaken the muddy water for chocolate milk.

The clank of shrinking pipes and swelling doors starts at lunchtime and subsides right after our 3 p.m. naps. The elders attribute the sound to our undeveloped mechanical ears. Years later, when we finally learn the truth about the noise, we forgive them for misleading us.

Inside an apartment room, a missing child pretends to be where the miniature circus toys sing with tinny voices.

Elsewhere in the building, a mother pretends to look for the missing child. The elders do not call the police until it is too late.

The First Horse Known to Men

after Sylwia Skubis's *Lonely*

Near the time the world was to end, we discovered your husk in the dump. We didn't know what to make of it. Your cogs were melted. The metallic mane that shone throughout the war had been reduced to coiled aluminum strips. We recognized the threaded joints that held you together. This was how people manufactured creatures like you.

The village idiot, who built airplanes in his youth, was the one who spoke your name: "Horse," he said.

The syllable was strange yet familiar. An articulation from history.

"Fine horse. Very fine horse. Our horse…ours." He was crying.

Nobody said anything.

I noticed Syria extracting your left radar eye. I was sure she'd spend nights studying it under artificial light.

Landlocked

after Jean-Marie Poumeyrol's *Bateau de sauvetage*
(2003)

You know it is just after the nuclear winter when the mutilated dogs sniff their paws for a whiff of their long-dead masters. You take turns distracting them otherwise they will turn on you or on one of your legless sisters. Then there are the giant dragonflies that follow you home after your daily search for kindling, and if you don't run fast enough, swoop in and pluck you off the ground. The best stories are supposed to be those about the end of the world. But that's until you discuss the details your townsfolk have swept under the rug: Mrs. Burdick refusing to surrender her left arm when it was her turn to give up something, how you stuff your pillows with morsels of the dead, how you buff every oil lamp, every fancy perfume bottle, every silvery gravy boat you come across in the landfill in search of the djinn that will change your life.

And when nobody's looking, you head to the glass arch of the greenhouse that the carnivorous plants haven't yet overtaken. The white birds, normal ones, shriek and rise in a flurry of molting feathers. There, in the middle, is the shape of your faith. For weeks, you have been rebuilding the ark you unearthed. For weeks, you have been praying for the flood.

Year of the Carnivores

after Martin Wittfooth's *Year of the Carnivore*

(2009)

oil on panel

12 × 16 in.

We let the second-generation creatures get away with it. They stole the wings off our butterflies so they could fly, so they could claim their share of what was left of the irradiated skies. We held our breath as they drank from the undulating pitcher plants, wishing we had long ago learned to adapt to the plants' predatory movements.

There should have been nothing in their caves that would allow them to grow. Only moss, exposed bedrock, volcanic debris, and small insects. But somehow, they did grow—stronger, more disfigured as they holed deeper inside the subterranean caverns.

It started with four missing village children. The creatures swore to never being near those kids, swore with their inch-long incisors and the yellowish glow in their eyes.

We believed them. Weeks later, we found the corpses in the marsh. The hair and nails were longer. The ribcages were ripped open. A bloodied butterfly wing was clutched in one of the dead children's hands.

The first of the creatures we killed during the weeklong hunt was unrecognizable. The darkness must have transformed it to the point that even its eyes, when fully open, were just pinpricks of light. In time, we realized that the second-generation creatures would outgrow their eyes. In time, they would have no need for sight. When they retreated from our spears, there was nothing inferior in their gait, nothing harmless in the protrusions on their stunted wings.

Strange City

after Dariusz Zawadzki's *Strange City*

(1997)

drawing

58 × 79 cm

One day we were ordered by the government to no longer pretend to be human. We stripped our clothes to reveal aging, gangrened skin. Our larvae-infested bed sores and cankered wounds, inflicted by monsters we disguised as domestic pets, bled in the open.

Everywhere we looked, we noticed unfolding. All the hummingbirds were vultures. All the dogs were grisly post-war mutations.

In search of sustenance, we prowled the streets of this strange city, and with each step, our emaciated forms left something behind: a portion of our scabbed flesh, a rotted limb. Someone always scrambled to collect it, to place it inside a toothless mouth, forever hoping that anything ingested would prevent death.

The car...

after Dariusz Zawadzki's *The car...*

(1998)

drawing

70 × 100 cm

Barefoot, my sisters and I took turns wheeling the husk of a baby in the stroller. The mummified infant, skeletonized hands still grasping an old-fashioned rattle, was one of the things we discovered in an obsolete incubator inside the factory.

We were all convinced that, in time, it would wake and come back to life like the dead that flocked to our neighborhood.

The baby's smell drew the flies and vultures—ancient creatures that were much larger than us. So to confuse them, we chose the path across the ransacked graveyard.

The Gathering

after Dariusz Zawadzki's *The Gathering*

(2002)

painting

90 × 100 cm

The city elders developed beaks instead of mouths. Yet they learned to walk upright and not on all fours. We had no idea whether or not they were human before they mutated.

Their bulging stomachs contained parasitic strains that exhaled the air we needed to exist. So we alternated between feeding them whatever offspring we could produce from our deformed genitalia and sacrificing one or two of the debilitated city inhabitants.

For what seemed like eons, we listened to their belching, their satisfied grunts.

What the Boatman Sees

after Monte Dolack's *Midnight All A Glimmer*

(2004)

acrylic on panel

16 × 20 in.

He stops paddling when he reaches the deepest part of the lake. He feels the currents underneath his flimsy boat. For once, he is lonely enough to hear the cold. The moon, he knows, will not last long. All afternoon, the fat radio has been singing about the end of the world, and soon his death will be more memorable than the others' in town. The slight curve of evening is shaped like a giant axe, and he is situated just inches to the left of this blade that will strike the lake's surface and fell the world.

Townscape

after Carel Willink's *Townscape*

(1934)

The best stories are always about the end of the world. This is one of those tales:

We were long gone after the nine-year drought; only our houses remained. The walls had yellowed on the sides facing the sun.

Mr. Allman's deli counter signboard was looted by a drifter in search of building materials. The scurvy-stricken scavenger did not live long enough. It was a shame. He was once a famous artist. *Had the dust been flowers, he would have swept them into crystal-cut vases behind the florist's window.*

At the edge of town, the church bells sometimes tolled. Perhaps, it was the wind. Perhaps, it was something else, something that survived and replaced us.

The first day of the rainy season arrived with the roar of a world just being made.

Mirage

after Soizick Meister's *Mirage*

12 × 12 in.

Whenever we dream during this eleven-year drought, we come up with this:

A man sits, drifting aimlessly on a makeshift barge. The waters, blue-green from this side of the world where we are trapped on the uppermost floors of whitewashed apartment buildings, taper into ripples. The closer the waves are to the horizon, the stronger they become. A dolphin leaps. The man applauds. Splashes of water everywhere. Hitting his balding head. Hitting his face. His laughter we hear over and over.

We Figure the Leaves

after René Magritte's *The Companions of Fear*

(1942)

oil on canvas

70.4 × 92 cm

We figure the leaves will find a way back inside the house, where they occupy more than their fair share of furniture. The smell of ruin and the lack of rain have not yet permeated. It must be what draws them to us, draws them indoors where we multiply when faced with extinction.

We figure the leaves will not do enough damage. They have the tiniest of hands that cringe at the feel of dust. Even when provoked, they remain harmless. Not once have they interrupted our sleep. It's like we are writing about life and drawing from an upturned hat the names of our enemies; we do not have to care whether or not the leaves exist. There is more to this room, this house, than the door that will not close to conceal the things dying inside.

Autumn, and they grit their teeth. Summer, and they explode in color. Winter, and we let them tiptoe their way to death.

We figure the leaves will leave us alone.

We figure the house has enough walls to keep them out.

They enter through gaps between the floorboards and under the doors. They clog and fatten the pipes, then escape from the toilet bowl. We take turns flushing, but the leaves are too many, too large as they congeal into familiar shapes. Exhausted, we flee the house our forefathers built with their own hands. It costs next to nothing to keep us alive inside the freezer or under the bed, yet they will not allow us to stay.

In time, the leaves assume our posture, talk, crease themselves beautiful in the eyes of other leaves. Hands scrunch together to turn on and off light switches, television remote controls, the triggers of hunting rifles. They rummage through our porn stash. They cook breakfast. They squabble and take desk jobs and cheat on their wives and taxes.

Outside the house, the trees, now leafless, are slowly drying. We shudder amid them. Under them.

End of the World

after René Magritte's *The Key to the Fields* or

La Clef de champs

(1936)

oil on canvas

80 × 60 cm

A day is loosened on its hinges. Bedridden by the flu, Justin crawls to the only window of his room and pounds his fist against the glass until it cracks.

Outside, the wind becomes desperate. It clings to every tree branch situated high enough to avoid the ground where the meteorologists lie in wait.

There are no birds; it is not normal to see them this time of year.

On the street across, the children are full of bulbous things to slide around. They laugh at Justin when they realize he is dying. They laugh at almost everything.

·Publication History·

These stories, some in earlier versions, first appeared or are forthcoming in the following publications:

Philippines Free Press: "The People of the Farm"
Mary Journal: "Bogomil's Landing"
Mary Journal: "Bogomil's Ceremonial Stage: Caspar and His Props"
Barge Journal: "Everything That Rises"
Barge Journal: "Self-Portrait as Sky Scraper"
Barge Journal: "Self-Portrait as Big House"
Gargoyle Magazine: "Abandoned Dwellings"
Contrary Magazine: "House and Men"
Exact Change Only: "Hope"
Everyday Weirdness: "Bad Egg"
Chômu Press - *Dadaoism* anthology: "Nowhere Room"
Prime Mincer: "Gregor Samsa Plays the Flute"
Connotation Press: "Man in a Black Suit"
Mary Journal: "Giorgio at the Piazza"
The Brooklyner: "Revenge of the Goldfish"
The Prose-Poem Project: "Startled Emu"

Mixer: "Obliterating the Outcast"

An Electric Tragedy: "The Perilous Compassion of the Honey Queen"

quiet Shorts: "Dangerous Liaisons"

Southword: "The Couple in Lace"

Barge Journal: "Birdcage"

Sou'wester: "Bad Love and Carnage" ("Bad Love")

Mixer: "The Village of the Mermaids"

Ping•Pong: "Self-Portrait as Netherworld"

Ping•Pong: "Self-Portrait as Roots"

Ping•Pong: "Self-Portrait as Fiery Skirt"

Sou'wester: "Sketch for a Dirty Princess"

Mixer: "The First Days of Spring"

Mixer: "Bug Chairs"

Third Wednesday: "One Story About Flight"

Third Wednesday: "Rivalerne and Shelving"

Dirtcakes: "Surgical Addiction"

Anobium: "A True Story"

The Yalobusha Review: "Nobody's Beast"

Every Day Fiction: "Flowers, Secrets"

Mixer: "Rain of Men"

Connotation Press: "Time Transfixed"

An Electric Tragedy: "The Walking Lesson"

Linger Fiction: "Underneath"

Linger Fiction: "The City is Landing" (Reprinted as a comic in *Schlock Magazine*)

Linger Fiction: "Attack at Dawn"

Connotation Press: "City of the Dead"

The Hiss Quarterly: "Inside the Calorimeter Cup" (Reprinted in *The Fringe Magazine*)

Eschatology: "As Long As You Burn"

Birkensnake: "Boy with a Propeller Head"

Eschatology: "Requiem for Industry" (A podcast in *Cast Macabre*)

Sonar 4 Ezine: "Shadow of a Boy" (Reprinted in *The Short Story Library*)

Connotation Press: "The Apartment Building Before It Was Torn Down"

Eschatology: "Landlocked" (A podcast in *The Way of the Buffalo*)

Tales of the Zombie War: "Year of the Carnivores"

The Lindenwood Review: "What the Boatman Sees"

Connotation Press: "Townscape"

Contrary Magazine: "Mirage"

Hobart: "We Figure the Leaves" (A podcast in *The Way of the Buffalo*)

Philistine Press (*Smaller Than Most* electronic chapbook): "Bad Egg," "The Collage Artist," "The Taxidermist and the Girls Made of Dead Things," and "Flowers, Secrets"

·Acknowledgments·

Many thanks to the editors of the following journals, magazines, and anthologies: *An Electric Tragedy, Anobium, Barge Journal, Birkensnake, Connotation Press, Contrary Magazine, Dadaism* anthology, *Dirtcakes, Eschatology, Every Day Fiction, Everyday Weirdness, Exact Change Only, Gargoyle Magazine, Hobart, Linger Fiction, Mary Journal, Mixer, Philippines Free Press,* Philistine Press, *Prime Mincer, quiet Shorts, Schlock Magazine, Sonar 4 Ezine, Southword, Sou'wester, Tales of the Zombie War, The Brooklyner, The Fringe Magazine, The Hiss Quarterly, The Lindenwood Review, The Prose-Poem Project, The Short Story Library, The Way of the Buffalo, The Yalobusha Review,* and *Third Wednesday.*

And to Erin McKnight who titled the collection and made sure that every word was in place.

Kristine Ong Muslim has authored many chapbooks, most recently *Night Fish* (Shoe Music Press/Elevated Books, 2011) and *Smaller Than Most* (Philistine Press, 2011). Forthcoming books include the full-length poetry collection *Grim Series* (Popcorn Press) and several print chapbooks.  Her short fiction and poetry have been published in hundreds of magazines, journals, and anthologies, including *Bellevue Literary Review*, *Boston Review*, *Contrary Magazine*, *Existere*, *Hobart*, *Narrative Magazine*, *Southword*, *Sou'wester*, *The Pedestal Magazine*, *Turnrow*, and *Verse Daily*. She has received multiple nominations for the Pushcart Prize, *Best of the Web 2011*, and the Science Fiction Poetry Association's Rhysling Award. Her work also has garnered several Honorable Mentions in *The Year's Best Fantasy and Horror*.

•Her online home is http://kristinemuslim.weebly.com•

CPSIA information can be obtained at www.ICGtesting.com
Printed in the USA
BVOW071424290212

284122BV00001B/26/P